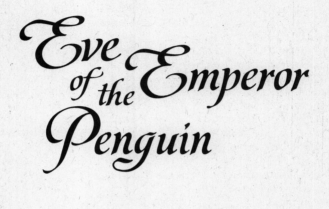

Eve of the Emperor Penguin

Magic Tree House® Books

#1: DINOSAURS BEFORE DARK
#2: THE KNIGHT AT DAWN
#3: MUMMIES IN THE MORNING
#4: PIRATES PAST NOON
#5: NIGHT OF THE NINJAS
#6: AFTERNOON ON THE AMAZON
#7: SUNSET OF THE SABERTOOTH
#8: MIDNIGHT ON THE MOON
#9: DOLPHINS AT DAYBREAK
#10: GHOST TOWN AT SUNDOWN
#11: LIONS AT LUNCHTIME
#12: POLAR BEARS PAST BEDTIME
#13: VACATION UNDER THE VOLCANO
#14: DAY OF THE DRAGON KING
#15: VIKING SHIPS AT SUNRISE
#16: HOUR OF THE OLYMPICS
#17: TONIGHT ON THE *TITANIC*
#18: BUFFALO BEFORE BREAKFAST
#19: TIGERS AT TWILIGHT
#20: DINGOES AT DINNERTIME
#21: CIVIL WAR ON SUNDAY
#22: REVOLUTIONARY WAR
    ON WEDNESDAY
#23: TWISTER ON TUESDAY
#24: EARTHQUAKE IN THE
    EARLY MORNING
#25: STAGE FRIGHT ON A
    SUMMER NIGHT
#26: GOOD MORNING, GORILLAS
#27: THANKSGIVING ON THURSDAY
#28: HIGH TIDE IN HAWAII

Merlin Missions

#29: CHRISTMAS IN CAMELOT
#30: HAUNTED CASTLE ON HALLOWS EVE
#31: SUMMER OF THE SEA SERPENT
#32: WINTER OF THE ICE WIZARD
#33: CARNIVAL AT CANDLELIGHT
#34: SEASON OF THE SANDSTORMS
#35: NIGHT OF THE NEW MAGICIANS
#36: BLIZZARD OF THE BLUE MOON
#37: DRAGON OF THE RED DAWN
#38: MONDAY WITH A MAD GENIUS
#39: DARK DAY IN THE DEEP SEA

Magic Tree House® Research Guides

DINOSAURS
KNIGHTS AND CASTLES
MUMMIES AND PYRAMIDS
PIRATES
RAIN FORESTS
SPACE
TITANIC
TWISTERS AND OTHER TERRIBLE STORMS
DOLPHINS AND SHARKS
ANCIENT GREECE AND THE OLYMPICS
AMERICAN REVOLUTION
SABERTOOTHS AND THE ICE AGE
PILGRIMS
ANCIENT ROME AND POMPEII
TSUNAMIS AND OTHER NATURAL DISASTERS
POLAR BEARS AND THE ARCTIC
SEA MONSTERS
 PENGUINS AND ANTARCTICA

MAGIC TREE HOUSE® #40
A MERLIN MISSION

Eve of the Emperor Penguin

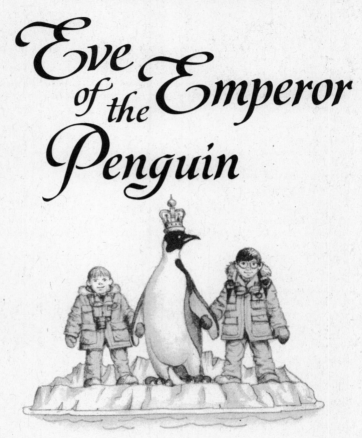

by Mary Pope Osborne

illustrated by Sal Murdocca

A STEPPING STONE BOOK™

Random House New York

Text copyright © 2008 by Mary Pope Osborne
Illustrations copyright © 2008 by Sal Murdocca

Published in the United States by Random House Children's Books, a division of Random House, Inc., New York.

Random House and colophon are registered trademarks and A Stepping Stone Book and colophon are trademarks of Random House, Inc. Magic Tree House is a registered trademark of Mary Pope Osborne; used under license.

Visit us on the Web!
www.magictreehouse.com
www.randomhouse.com/kids

Educators and librarians, for a variety of teaching tools, visit us at
www.randomhouse.com/teachers

Library of Congress Cataloging-in-Publication Data
Osborne, Mary Pope.
Eve of the emperor penguin / by Mary Pope Osborne ; illustrated by Sal Murdocca. — 1st ed.
   p. cm.
Summary: The magic tree house takes Jack and Annie to Antarctica to search for the fourth secret of happiness for Merlin.
ISBN 978-0-375-83733-3 (trade) — ISBN 978-0-375-93733-0 (lib. bdg.) —
ISBN 978-0-375-83734-0 (pbk.)
[1. Tree houses—Fiction. 2. Voyages and travels—Fiction. 3. Magic—Fiction.
4. Brothers and sisters—Fiction. 5. Antarctica—Fiction.]
I. Murdocca, Sal, ill. II. Title.
PZ7.O81167Ev 2008 [Fic]—dc22 2008005769

Printed in the United States of America

10 9 8 7 6 5 4 3 2

First Edition

For Nory van Rhyn,
who reminds me of Penny

Dear Reader,

For many years, one of my favorite places to visit has been the Central Park Zoo in New York City. My husband, Will, and I love going there for one main reason: to visit the building where about sixty gentoo and chinstrap penguins live. The penguins always make us laugh—especially when they jump out of the water onto the edge of their pool. We also love watching their keepers call each penguin by name and hand-feed fish to them.

While I was writing this book, I combined my memories of watching the penguins at the zoo with my research on Antarctica. And I used my imagination to think about Jack and Annie searching for a secret of happiness to share with Merlin. I always mix these three things together to create a Magic Tree House book: <u>memory, research,</u> and <u>imagination</u>. But there's one other ingredient that goes into my work on this series: _joy_. I love to write—and I love sharing Jack and Annie's adventures with you. That's one of my own personal secrets of happiness.

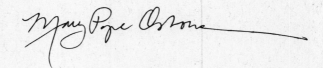

CONTENTS

"Glittering white, shining blue, raven black;
in the light of the sun the land looks like a fairy tale."

—Roald Amundsen,
the first explorer to reach
the South Pole, 1911

Prologue

One summer day in Frog Creek, Pennsylvania, a mysterious tree house appeared in the woods. A brother and sister named Jack and Annie soon learned that the tree house was magic—it could take them to any time and any place in history. They also learned that the tree house belonged to Morgan le Fay, a magical librarian from the legendary realm of Camelot.

After Jack and Annie traveled on many adventures for Morgan, Merlin the magician began sending them on "Merlin Missions" in the tree house. With help from two young sorcerers named Teddy and Kathleen, Jack and Annie visited four mythical places and found valuable objects to help save Camelot.

For their next four Merlin Missions, Jack and Annie were told they must travel to real times and real places in history and prove to Merlin that they could use magic wisely.

Now Jack and Annie must save Merlin himself. Morgan le Fay has asked them to find four secrets of happiness to help Merlin out of a deep sadness. Having found the first three secrets, they are waiting to find out where they are going to search for the fourth. . . .

CHAPTER ONE

Smile

Jack was raking leaves on a chilly November afternoon. Geese honked overhead.

"Smile," said Annie.

Annie was pointing her camera at him. "No pictures now," he said.

"Come on," said Annie. "Smile!"

Jack gave her a goofy smile.

"A *real* one," said Annie. "I'm taking pictures for our family project at school."

Jack crossed his eyes and made his smile even goofier.

"Okay. Be that way," said Annie. "I'm going into the woods."

"Good," said Jack. "Go."

"Maybe the tree house is back," said Annie.

"You always say that when you want me to stop what I'm doing and do something with you," said Jack.

"Maybe Teddy and Kathleen are waiting for us," said Annie.

"Yeah, yeah, yeah," said Jack.

"Maybe today's the day they want us to look for a fourth secret of happiness for Merlin," said Annie. "Maybe they're going to send us to a super-cool place."

"Good. Hope they do. Have fun," said Jack. "I want to finish raking these leaves before dark." He glanced up at the late-afternoon sky—just in time to see a bright streak of light pass over the Frog Creek woods. "Whoa!" Jack turned to Annie with a smile. "Did you see that?"

"Hold that smile!" said Annie as she took Jack's picture. "Thanks! Perfect."

"But did you see that?" Jack asked. "The light going over the woods?"

"Ha-ha," said Annie.

"No, I'm serious! It was a bright light! Wait a second!" Jack put down his rake and dashed into the house. "Mom! Dad!" he shouted. "Annie and I are going for a walk, okay?"

"Okay," called their dad, "but be home before dark!"

"And wear your scarves and hats!" called their mom.

"We will!" Jack grabbed their scarves, their hats, and his backpack from the hall closet and ran back outside. "Let's go!" he said to Annie.

Annie put her camera in her jacket pocket and took off running with Jack. They ran up the sidewalk, crossed the street, and headed into the shadowy Frog Creek woods. They crunched over a carpet of fallen leaves until they came to the tallest tree.

The magic tree house was there! Kathleen and Teddy were looking out the window. The two young enchanters were both wearing dark cloaks.

"Hi! Hi!" Annie shouted.

"We were about to come looking for you!" said Kathleen. "How did you know we were here?"

"I saw the light!" said Jack.

"Climb up!" said Teddy.

Jack and Annie hurried up the rope ladder. When they climbed inside the tree house, they hugged Teddy and Kathleen.

"Is it time to go on another mission?" said Annie.

"Indeed," said Kathleen.

"And it is quite urgent now," said Teddy.

"Merlin is failing quickly," said Kathleen. She blinked back tears.

"Oh, no!" said Annie.

"Morgan wants you to find the final secret of happiness *today*," said Teddy. "And then you must return to Camelot to present all four secrets to Merlin. You remember the first three, do you not?"

"Sure!" said Jack. "We have three gifts to help us remember. I kept them in my backpack."

"A poem, a drawing, and a seashell," said Annie.

"Good," said Teddy. "Here is where you will look for the final secret." He took a book from his cloak and handed it to Jack.

On the cover was a picture of a volcano surrounded by snow and ice. The title said:

"Antarctica?" said Jack. "We studied Antarctica in school. There's hardly anything there.

Where would we find a secret of happiness in Antarctica?"

"I do not know," said Kathleen. "But Morgan has sent a rhyme to help your search." She handed Annie a slip of parchment.

Annie read Morgan's rhyme aloud:

> *For the final secret, you must go*
> *To a burning mountain of ice and snow*
> *On wheels, by air, then all fall down,*
> *Till you come to the Cave of the Ancient Crown.*
> *Then speed to Camelot by close of day,*
> *Lest grief take Merlin forever away.*

"Forever away?" said Annie.

"I fear so," said Teddy.

"I don't understand," said Jack. "This rhyme sounds like we're going to a fantasy world, a place with 'a burning mountain' and a 'Cave of the Ancient Crown.' But Antarctica's a real place, totally real."

"Aye, Morgan's rhyme is a mystery to me, too," said Teddy.

"But you still have the Wand of Dianthus to help you, do you not?" asked Kathleen.

"Yes," said Jack. But he looked inside his backpack just to make sure. There it was: the gleaming spiraled wand of the unicorn.

"Good," said Kathleen. "And you remember the three rules of the wand?"

"Sure," said Annie. "The wand's magic only works if our wish is for the good of others. It only works after we've tried our hardest. And it only works if our wish is *five* words."

"Excellent," said Teddy.

"I wish you guys could come with us," said Jack.

"We must return to Morgan and try to help Merlin," said Kathleen. "But with your courage and intelligence, I know you will be able to find the secret by yourselves."

Jack nodded, embarrassed. But Kathleen's words did make him feel more confident.

"And after you have found it, you must hurry to meet us in Camelot," said Teddy. "Just point to the word 'Camelot' on the rhyme from Morgan and make a wish to go there."

"Got it," said Annie.

"Go now. Quickly," said Kathleen. "And good luck."

"See you soon," said Annie.

Jack took a deep breath, then pointed to the cover of the book. "I wish we could go there!" he said.

The wind started to blow.

The tree house started to spin.

It spun faster and faster.

Then everything was still.

Absolutely still.

CHAPTER TWO

Lots of Ice

"Welcome to Antarctica," said Annie.

Jack and Annie were bundled in cold-weather gear. They both wore snow pants, gloves, boots with spikes, and thick red parkas with hoods. Goggles covered their eyes, and wool masks covered their mouths and noses. A hiker's backpack had replaced Jack's own pack.

Jack felt trapped by all the gear. He pulled his mask down under his chin and pushed his goggles onto his forehead. Annie did the same. Their breath made clouds of mist in the freezing air.

"It's really cold here!" said Jack. The wind stung his bare face and made his eyes water. But he kept his mask and goggles off as he looked out the window with Annie.

The tree house was on the ground. It was tucked under the overhang of an ice cliff near the ocean. Icy seawater sparkled in the sunlight. The shore was silent and deserted.

"It looks totally empty out there," said Jack. "I still don't get it—how do we find the Cave of the Ancient Crown here? No king or queen ever ruled Antarctica. In fact, no people ever lived here at all until explorers came in recent times."

"Let's get started and try to figure it all out," said Annie.

"Not so fast," said Jack. He pulled off his glove and opened their research book to the first chapter. He read aloud:

> **The continent of Antarctica is the coldest, driest, and windiest place on earth. Larger in area than the United States, it is a land filled with ice—ice cliffs, icebergs, ice sheets, ice shelves—**

"Okay, lots of ice," said Annie. "Got it. Let's *go*."

"In a minute." Jack kept reading:

> **But Antarctica was not always a land of ice. Eons ago, it was part of a supercontinent scientists have named**

Gondwana. It had forests, flowers, and
many animals, including dinosaurs. But
no people ever lived there.

"See?" said Jack. "No kings, no queens, no
crowns."

"Yep, let's go," said Annie.

But Jack kept reading:

Over millions of years, Antarctica broke
off from Gondwana and drifted south.

"Okay, I'm drifting now myself, Jack," said
Annie. "Byeee—" She climbed out the window
and disappeared from the tree house.

Jack looked back at the book, but before he
could read further, he heard Annie whoop with
laughter. "Oh, wow! Jack, come look!" she yelled.

"What is it?" said Jack, closing the book.

"You won't believe this!" said Annie. "You
have to come see!"

Jack put his glove back on and pulled on his
backpack. He folded the paper with Morgan's

rhyme and put it in his pocket. Then, clutching the research book to his chest, he climbed out of the window.

Jack followed the sound of Annie's laughter beyond the tree house. On the frozen seashore was a group of penguins, grown-ups and babies. The grown-ups had orange streaks on their cheeks, puffy white chests, and black wings they held straight by their sides. The babies were fluffy balls of gray fuzz. All the penguins were waddling toward Annie. They rocked from side to side, taking funny little steps.

Jack burst out laughing. The big penguins looked like a committee of little men in black suits.

The group stopped in front of Annie and squawked at her.

"Hi, guys," said Annie. "Glad to meet you!"

The penguins stared back at her with friendly curiosity.

"They're so cool," said Jack. He opened the

book and found a picture that looked like the group of penguins around Annie. He read:

> **Emperor penguins are the tallest and heaviest of the penguin species and are also the most ancient. Over three feet tall, grown penguins can weigh up to ninety pounds. Researchers say the penguin's closest ancestors lived 40 million years ago.**

"Forty million years!" said Jack. "So what time have we gone back to? A million years ago? A thousand years ago?"

"I don't know," said Annie. "But I'll take a picture of them for my family project. They look like a little family, don't they?" She pulled her camera out of her pocket and aimed it at the penguins. "Smile, everyone."

As Annie took a picture, a shadow moved over the ice. The penguins squawked loudly and clustered together.

Jack and Annie looked up. The shadow

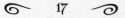

belonged to a giant bird circling above them. The bird was brownish gray with a long beak. It let out an eerie cry.

"What is that?" Annie asked with alarm.

"I'll look it up," said Jack. He flipped through the pages of their book to find a photo. "Here!" He read quickly:

> **Giant petrels are the vultures of Antarctica. They eat dead birds and animals. Sometimes they even attack young seals and pen—**

"Oh, no!" cried Annie.

Jack looked up. The petrel was diving toward the penguins. It hit the smallest one with its wing and swooped back into the air.

The penguin squawked and waddled away from the group. The petrel spread its wide wings and dove again.

"NO!" Annie cried.

The petrel swooped away but circled back toward them.

Jack dropped the book and scooped up a hand-
ful of snow to make a snowball. Before he could
throw it, the petrel attacked again. Jack leapt
toward the small penguin. He fell on his knees and
threw his arms around the fluffy little body.

Annie charged at the petrel. "Go! Get out of here!" she yelled, waving her arms.

The petrel cawed, then rose high into the sky and disappeared over the ice cliff.

Jack let go of the small penguin and stood up. The penguin peeped and waggled its head at Jack.

Jack laughed. "You're welcome," he said. "Now go back to your family. Go—"

He shooed the penguin back to the group. "All of you guys, back in the water now. You'll be safer there. Go, go."

The penguins squawked and flapped their wings as if saying good-bye. Then they waddled across the icy shore, taking quick, tiny steps toward the sea. One after another, they dove between cracks in the ice until they all disappeared.

"Bye, guys," said Annie.

HONK!

"What's that?" said Jack.

HONK!

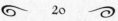

"It sounds like some kind of horn," said Annie.

"That's weird," said Jack.

"It's coming from over there," said Annie.

Jack picked up their book and followed Annie up the side of an icy slope. The metal spikes on his boots dug into the ice and kept him from slipping. When he and Annie reached the top, they looked down.

"Oh, man," said Jack. "We haven't gone back in time at all!"

CHAPTER THREE

Short Grown-ups

In the icy field below the slope were yellow, brown, and green buildings; telephone poles; metal pipes; and storage tanks. Tractors and bulldozers moved along gravel roads. It looked like a small town.

HONK! The sound came from a red bus with gigantic wheels that was parked nearby.

"What *is* this place?" asked Annie.

Jack looked in their book and found a photo that looked like the scene below. The caption read: *McMurdo Station.* Jack read the paragraph under the photo:

Antarctica has many scientific research stations, representing countries from all over the world. The largest is named McMurdo Station. Researchers live there for weeks or even months at a time.

HONK!

Jack looked up. He saw four people come out of a yellow building and start toward the bus. They were all bundled in red parkas with hoods, goggles, and masks. They carried backpacks and camera bags.

"They must be researchers," said Jack.

"Let's go talk to them," said Annie.

"We can't," said Jack. "They'll ask why two kids are traveling alone in Antarctica."

"Maybe they won't know we're kids," said Annie. "If we put our goggles and masks back on, we'll look just like them, only shorter. They'll think we're short grown-ups."

"Uh . . . I don't think so," said Jack.

Just then someone jumped off the bus. "Hi,

folks!" a woman shouted to the four researchers. "I'm Nancy—your bus driver and guide today!"

Nancy caught sight of Jack and Annie. She waved her arms at them. "Hello!" she called. "Are you two part of the group going up to the volcano?" She pointed toward a mountain looming in the distance.

"Did you hear that?" Jack said to Annie. "A volcano!" He cupped his gloved hands around his mouth. "Yes!" he shouted back in his deepest voice. "We're coming!"

"We are?" Annie asked with surprise.

"A *volcano*—get it?" said Jack. "A volcano is 'a burning mountain'!"

"Oh, right!" said Annie. "Like in the rhyme— the burning mountain! Got it!"

"Quick, cover up your face!" said Jack.

Jack and Annie covered their eyes with their goggles and pulled up their face masks. Then they started walking toward the bus.

"Try not to talk to anyone unless we have to,"

Jack said quickly. "And if we do, talk in a really deep voice."

"No problem," Annie croaked in a really deep voice.

"Um . . . maybe you shouldn't talk at all," said Jack.

"Hurry!" Nancy called to them.

"Coming!" Jack shouted in his deepest voice, and they started running across the snow.

By the time Jack and Annie arrived at the bus, everyone but Nancy had climbed aboard. "Good. You made it just in time!" Nancy said. "Follow me!" She bounded up the steep steps of the red bus and sat in the driver's seat.

Without a word, Jack and Annie climbed on after Nancy. Walking down the aisle, Jack glanced at the others in the group. A couple of them nodded and he nodded back. Everyone was hidden behind goggles, ski masks, and bulky parkas. Jack couldn't tell anyone's age, or even whether they were male or female.

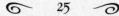

Jack and Annie sat a few rows behind the others. Jack took off his backpack and put it at his feet.

"All set?" Nancy asked, looking in the bus mirror.

Jack and Annie nodded.

Nancy closed the door and started the engine. As the bus's giant wheels moved slowly over the gravel road, Jack looked out the window.

The sun shone brightly on the wide, snowy fields. Glittering ice crystals blew in the wind. All the world around them seemed to be sparkling.

"How's everyone doing?" Nancy called over her shoulder. "Are you all happy campers?"

Everyone, including Jack and Annie, nodded.

"Good. I like travelers who don't complain!" Nancy joked.

So far, so good, Jack thought. No one seemed to suspect they were kids.

"We have a short ride," said Nancy. "But enough time for you all to introduce yourselves to

me. I'm Nancy Tyler, and I work here in Antarctica as a guide, a bus driver, and a flight
mechanic."

"Cool," whispered Annie.

"I know you all come from different countries
as researchers and journalists," said Nancy. "Start
from the front and tell me who you are."

The woman in front pulled down her face mask.
"I'm Lucy Banks," she said. "I'm an American,
and I'm a space scientist. I'm writing a paper on
the use of robots on the crater of Mount Erebus.
Hopefully this will help our work on Mars someday."

Oh, brother, thought Jack. *What can we say?
That we're Jack and Annie from Frog Creek and
we've come to Antarctica to find the fourth secret
of happiness to save Merlin the magician in
Camelot?*

"Wonderful, Lucy!" Nancy said. "Antarctica is
as similar to Mars as any place you can find on
earth. Next?"

"Ali Khan, biologist from Turkey," said the man sitting behind Lucy Banks. "I'm researching heat-resistant bacteria in the crater of Mount Erebus."

Quick, think! thought Jack.

"Very good!" said Nancy. "Next?"

"Tony Sars from Sydney, Australia," another man said. "I'm a travel writer for the *Sydney Morning Herald*." He held up a notebook.

"Good!" said Nancy.

Yes! thought Jack. He yanked off a glove and

pulled his notebook and a pencil out of his back-pack.

"Kim Lee," said the woman sitting behind Tony. "I'm a photographer for a Korean magazine."

"Great," said Nancy. "And my friends in the back?"

Without taking off his mask, Jack shouted in a deep voice, "*Frog Creek Times*, USA!" He held up his notebook. "Story about Antarctica. She's . . . uh . . ."

Annie held up her camera. "His photographer!" she called in a deep voice.

"Excellent!" said Nancy. "A great group! We'll hear more introductions later. Now, I know you've all heard this before, but I have to tell you again. It is very important to remember the rules here in Antarctica."

Jack opened his notebook and got ready to write down the rules.

"Never rush," said Nancy. "You should always think about where you're going and what you're doing."

Jack scribbled:

Go slow!

"Never walk on snow and ice fields alone," said Nancy. "In many places beneath the snow, there are deep, hidden cracks in the ice."

Jack wrote:

Stay with others!
Cracks in ice!

"And remember, all of Antarctica is a nature preserve," said Nancy. "*Never, ever* touch or disturb the wildlife."

"Oops," said Annie.

Jack frowned. "We really broke the rules with those penguins," he whispered.

"I know, but we won't do it again," Annie whispered back.

"Right," said Jack. He wrote down:

Never touch wildlife!

"Got all that?" Nancy asked the group.

Everyone nodded.

"Good," said Nancy. "I look forward to sharing Antarctica with you today. I know you'll all find some great information and stories!"

As the bus rolled along, no one gave Jack and Annie a second look. "Nancy called us 'friends,' " Jack whispered to Annie. "The others must think she knows us."

"Yeah, and *she* thinks we're friends with *them*," said Annie.

"We're getting away with this," said Jack. He could hardly believe it.

"It reminds me of our last mission," Annie whispered, "on the ship with the ocean scientists."

"This is better," said Jack. "Here everyone's treating us like grown-ups, and I don't feel like throwing up."

"And nowadays women get to do really cool stuff, too, like men do," said Annie.

"Good point," said Jack. "But there's still stuff about our rhyme I don't get." He pulled the rhyme out of his pocket, and he and Annie read it silently:

> *For the final secret, you must go*
> *To a burning mountain of ice and snow*
> *On wheels, by air, then all fall down,*
> *Till you come to the Cave of the Ancient Crown.*
> *Then speed to Camelot by close of day,*
> *Lest grief take Merlin forever away.*

"See, it sounds like it's talking about a magical world," said Jack. "But Antarctica is a hundred percent real. It's filled with scientists!"

"I know, but some of the rhyme fits," said Annie. "Like you said, the 'burning mountain of ice and snow' is the volcano, Mount Erebus." She pointed out the window of the bus. "And there it is."

A white mountain loomed in the distance. Ice and snow covered its slopes, and puffs of smoke rose from its peak, drifting into the blue sky.

"It's burning, all right," said Jack.

"And we're *on wheels*," said Annie.

"Yep," said Jack. He looked at the rhyme again. "Okay, 'burning mountain of ice and snow,' 'on wheels'—but then what about 'by air'? What's—"

"Oh, my gosh!" said Annie, craning her neck.

"What?" said Jack.

"Look over there!" said Annie.

CHAPTER FOUR

Happy Campers

Touching down onto a flat, snowy field was an orange and white helicopter. The helicopter had skis on the bottom so it could land on the ice and snow. The bus came to a stop at the edge of the field.

"We must be going to the volcano in a helicopter!" said Annie.

"*By air!* Just like the rhyme says!" said Jack. "Great!" Jack had always wanted to fly in a helicopter!

Nancy stood up. "For those of you getting off

the bus now, please remember," she said, "the helicopter blades are extremely dangerous. Always wait for a signal from the pilot before approaching the chopper."

Everyone watched as the spinning blades slowly came to a stop. The pilot waved from the helicopter window.

"Okay, Pete says we can go!" said Nancy.

Jack put their rhyme back into his pocket. He pulled on his backpack. Then, carrying his notebook and pencil, he filed down the aisle after Annie and the others who would join them in the helicopter. They all scrambled off the bus into the dazzling sunlight.

"Jump aboard!" said Nancy.

Jack and Annie followed the four other adults up the steps of the helicopter and squeezed into a small cabin. Sitting in two rows of seats behind the pilot, everyone buckled their seat belts.

Nancy pulled the door shut and turned the latch. Then she sat next to Pete and put on a set of headphones. "Headphones on, everyone! They're under your seats," she said. "They'll protect your ears from the chopper noise, and also serve as a radio so I can talk to you."

Everyone reached under their seats and took out headphones. Jack and Annie pulled off their hoods. Without taking off their goggles or face masks, they placed the headphones over their ears. The thick pads muffled the sounds around them.

Jack heard Nancy's voice over his headphones: "Testing, one, two, three. Can everyone hear me?"

Everyone nodded.

"Okay, Pete, take us to Mount Erebus!"

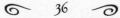

Pete the pilot started the helicopter. Even with his headphones on, Jack heard the roaring of the engine and the spinning of the blades. He held his breath as the chopper trembled and lifted off the ice and snow.

The helicopter shook and tilted. Then it buzzed forward through the blue sky.

Annie aimed her camera out the window and took pictures. The Korean photographer did the same, and the Australian journalist scribbled in his notebook.

Jack was too excited to take notes now. *This is great,* he thought. *All the words in the rhyme are coming true.* As they flew toward the burning mountain of ice and snow, he tried to remember what words came next. He slipped the rhyme out of his pocket and read:

> *. . . you must go*
> *To a burning mountain of ice and snow*
> *On wheels, by air, then all fall down . . .*

"All fall down"? Wait a minute. What does that *mean?* thought Jack. *Does that mean the chopper falls down? Do we fall out of the chopper?*

As these thoughts swirled through Jack's mind, Annie turned and gave him a thumbs-up.

Jack didn't want to scare her, so he nodded and shoved the rhyme back in his pocket. He watched anxiously out the window as the chopper approached a bright orange-red circle on top of Mount Erebus.

"Below is one of the world's most famous lava lakes," said Nancy over the headphones.

The chopper hovered motionless above the crater of the volcano. The lava lake bubbled and boiled. "That burning lava is miles deep," said Nancy. "Its temperature is over seventeen hundred degrees Fahrenheit. Can you guys on this side see okay? Pete?"

Pete tilted the helicopter to one side and then the other. Everyone but Jack oohed and aahed. Kim Lee and Annie took pictures.

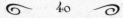

Go! thought Jack. *Before we all fall down!*

"Okay, Pete, that's great," said Nancy. "Let's land at the lower field camp now!"

The helicopter tilted upright and began moving down the side of the volcanic mountain. Jack saw a small orange building sticking up from the snow. Colorful snowmobiles were parked near it.

Moments later, the chopper touched down onto the slope. It rocked and shuddered, then came to a stop. *Whew,* thought Jack. They'd landed without falling from the sky into a burning lava lake. But then what could "all fall down" in the rhyme mean?

"Stay seated till the blades come to a *complete* stop!" said Nancy.

Everyone remained in their seats with their seat belts and headphones on.

"As you know, we'll be driving our snowmobiles up to the summit," said Nancy. "Driving a snowmobile can be very dangerous on these steep, icy slopes. Please remember everything you learned in your snowmobile training yesterday."

As the others nodded, Annie nodded, too. Jack nudged her. They'd never had any training with snowmobiles!

"Another warning," said Nancy. "I know you've also been training this week to prevent altitude sickness. But still—it can be very dangerous. So please let me know if you feel any symptoms."

Altitude sickness? Jack wondered. He pulled off his glove again and opened up his backpack. He took out the research book and looked up *altitude sickness* in the index. He turned to the right page and read:

> **Altitude sickness,** also known as *mountain sickness,* is caused by a lack of oxygen at great heights. Symptoms include headaches, dizziness, and shortness of breath. Climbers traveling up Mount Erebus train for days by climbing to gradually increasing heights.

Oh, no, thought Jack.

The spinning of the helicopter blades had come to a stop.

"Okay, happy campers," said Nancy. "All clear! Before we drive up to the top, we'll gather in the hut!"

Nancy opened the helicopter door. Everyone took off their headphones, undid their seat belts, and followed her down the steps of the chopper. Jack was last as he struggled with putting the research book away, getting his glove back on, and then pulling his pack onto his back.

"What took you so long?" Annie asked when he got out of the chopper.

Jack just shook his head.

"Have a safe trip back to the station, Pete!" called Nancy. "See you later!"

Pete waved from the window. Then the chopper blades started rotating again. The chopper lifted off the ground and thundered away.

CHAPTER FIVE

Lava Bombs

Jack didn't feel like a happy camper anymore. Walking through the cold, thin air, he looked at the snowmobiles parked near the hut.

"We don't know how to drive snowmobiles!" Jack whispered to Annie. "We haven't trained for anything, including altitude sickness!"

"That's okay. If we get in trouble, we can use the wand," said Annie.

"No, we can't," said Jack. "We can't use the wand just for ourselves. Plus, we haven't tried our hardest yet."

"This way, gang," called Nancy. She was ushering everyone into the small orange building.

Jack and Annie followed the group inside. The one-room hut had plastic chairs, a small heater, axes, jugs of water, and shelves with boxes of trail mix.

"Have a seat and help yourself to some of the best water in the world," Nancy said. "It comes from melted glacier ice."

Everyone sat on the plastic chairs. Lucy, Kim, Tony, and Ali poured water into tin cups and lowered their masks to drink. Jack was thirsty, but he shook his head *no* at Annie. He was afraid for them to show their faces.

"Before we take off, I want to warn you again about the snowmobiles," said Nancy. "No matter how much training you've had, you must be very careful. On your ride up to the crater, remember to drive sideways so if the snowmobile slips and rolls over, your leg won't get crushed."

Everyone nodded.

How do you drive sideways? Jack wondered in a panic.

"Don't be afraid to go fast, and don't lock up the brakes," said Nancy. "Locking your brakes can spell disaster."

"And watch out for lava bombs," said Ali, the biologist.

"Lava bombs?" Jack piped. He quickly cleared his throat and deepened his voice. "Excuse me. Lava bombs?"

"Lava that spits from the crater," said Ali.

"Spits?" repeated Jack.

"Like oatmeal that bubbles and spatters out of the pot," said Lucy, the space scientist.

"Except these bombs aren't made of oatmeal," said Ali. "They're blobs of fiery hot liquid rock. Some of them can be as big as a car. They burn deep holes in the ice and snow."

"If they hit you . . . ," said Tony, chuckling. "Well, just think about it."

Jack didn't want to think about it.

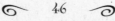

"Seriously, it's pretty neat," said Nancy. "For millions of years, hot gas and lava have carved deep, hidden places beneath the surface ice of these slopes—caverns and towers. No one knows all the secrets of Mount Erebus."

Nancy took a last sip of water and put her cup down. "Okay, guys, you have a few hours to do your experiments and get your stories. Then Pete will come back for us. Let's go!"

As Jack stood up to go, he almost fell over. The room was spinning. He closed his eyes, but that only made it worse. After the others had filed out the door, Jack sat back down on his chair. *I'll just stay here for a second*, he thought, his heart pounding.

"You okay?" said Annie, coming back into the hut.

"I'm dizzy," said Jack, trying to catch his breath. "I think I've got altitude sickness."

"I don't feel so great, either," said Annie. "Try taking off your mask and goggles so you can

breathe better." She helped Jack lift off his mask and goggles. "Does that help?"

"Yeah, a little. . . ." Jack took a deep breath. "But we need *lots* of help."

"What do you mean?" said Annie.

"Help getting over altitude sickness," said Jack, "help driving snowmobiles, help dodging lava bombs, help finding an ancient crown . . . and what is *that*, anyway—an *ancient crown*?"

Nancy poked her head back into the hut. "What's up, guys? You coming?"

"Yikes," said Annie.

Jack quickly tried to put his goggles and mask back on. But it was too late.

"What—what are you—who are you?" Nancy sputtered. "You're not a journalist! You're a kid!"

"Don't worry," said Annie in a deep voice. "He's my son."

"*What?*" said Nancy.

"He is," said Annie. "I often take him on my assignments."

"*You what?*" said Nancy.

"Annie, give it up," said Jack. "We're caught."

"Oh, okay," said Annie. She pushed up her goggles and pulled down her mask. "I'm Annie, and he's Jack. We're sister and brother."

"I'm going to have a heart attack!" said Nancy. "What are you kids doing here?"

"We were looking for . . ." Annie stopped. "Um . . ." Jack knew even Annie couldn't explain their mission to save Merlin to Nancy.

"This is unbelievable!" said Nancy. "I've got to get you two back to the station! Your parents must be frantic. I can't believe this!"

"No, no, it's our fault. No one will blame *you*," said Jack.

But Nancy was pulling out a small radio. "Come in, Pete. Come in."

The radio crackled and popped. Then Pete's voice came through. "Hear you, Nancy," he said.

"Pete, you need to get the chopper back here quick and pick up two of my group. They're just little kids!"

Not so little, thought Jack.

"Repeat that, Nancy," said Pete.

"Two little kids came with the group!" Nancy shouted. "I didn't know they were kids—oh, it's too hard to explain! Can you come back right away, please?"

"Sure thing," said Pete. "You head up with the others. I'll pick up the kids."

"Thanks. They'll be here at the hut, waiting for you to take them back," said Nancy. "Over and out."

CHAPTER SIX

All Fall Down

Nancy put away her radio and looked at Jack and Annie. "I don't know how you two got past me."

"We're sorry," said Annie.

"This is unbelievable!" said Nancy.

Jack couldn't believe it, either. How did they mess up so badly?

"I'm so sorry I brought you here," said Nancy.

"No, no, it's *our* fault," Jack said again.

"It's mine, all mine, oh . . . ," said Nancy. She seemed near tears. "You're just little kids."

Not so little! thought Jack again. *Gee!*

A snowmobile rumbled outside, its engine warming up.

"Oh, dear," said Nancy. "I've got to lead the group up a safe route to the crater, or they'll be in trouble. But Pete should be back here in just a few minutes. Will you be okay by yourselves till then?"

"We'll be fine, don't worry," said Annie.

"Good," said Nancy. "Here, sweeties." She poured some water into two cups and gave them to Jack and Annie. "Drink." While they drank the water, Nancy spread a blanket on the floor and turned on the small heater.

"Lie down here," she said. "Just rest." She patted the blanket.

Jack and Annie lay down. Nancy covered them with another blanket. "If you get thirsty, drink more water," she said.

"Thanks," said Annie. Jack was too embarrassed to say anything. He felt like a preschool kid being put down for a nap.

"Okay!" Nancy said with a big sigh. "You kids nearly gave me a heart attack," she repeated half to herself as she left the hut.

"Sorry," said Jack.

But Nancy was gone.

Soon the roar and rumble of the snowmobiles filled the air as Nancy led the scientists and journalists up the mountain.

"We really messed up our mission this time," said Jack, lying under the blanket.

"And we were doing so well, too," said Annie. She sat up. "Can I see Morgan's rhyme, please?"

Jack pulled the rhyme out of his pocket and handed it to Annie.

"Okay," said Annie. She read aloud:

> *. . . then all fall down,*
> *Till you come to the Cave of the Ancient Crown.*

"I wonder if *this* counts as falling down?" asked Annie. She put the rhyme into her pocket.

"I don't think so," said Jack. "I don't know what that means. And there's no 'Ancient Crown' in Antarctica. It's all science and research and rules and helicopters and snowmobiles. . . . It's the real world. . . ." His voice trailed off.

"Well, I know one thing: I don't want to waste time lying around here," said Annie. She threw off the blanket and stood up. "At least I can take a few pictures while we wait for Pete."

"You really feel like doing that?" said Jack.

"Not really, but I'm going to try," said Annie.

"I don't think you should," said Jack.

"Don't worry, I'll be back soon," said Annie. "Maybe I'll see an ancient crown."

"Yeah, sure," said Jack.

Annie put on her goggles and ski mask and headed outside.

Jack reached into his pack and pulled out their book. He took off his glove and looked up *ancient crown* in the index. He wasn't surprised to find it wasn't there.

Jack put the book back in his pack and took out his notebook. He read over his notes:

Go slow!
Stay with others!
Cracks in ice!
Never touch wildlife!

Jack's hand was cold, so he put his glove back on. He put away his notebook, and then laid his head back down and closed his eyes. He just wanted to sleep. The warmth from the small heater felt good. The sound of the snowmobiles was fading into the distance. As he started to fall asleep, the words of his notes ran through his mind: *Go slow. . . . Stay with others. . . . Cracks in ice. . . .*

Oh, no! thought Jack. He sat straight up. He tossed off the blanket. He threw on his pack and rushed out of the hut.

The wind was blowing the snow into icy clouds. Jack pulled up his ski mask and lowered his goggles. "Annie!" he shouted.

"What?" Her voice came from the distance.

Jack caught sight of her. She was aiming her camera up the slope at the smoking crater of the mountain.

"You have to come back now!" he shouted, walking toward her. "You shouldn't be walking around by yourself!"

"Okay, okay." Annie put her camera in her pocket.

"Come on," said Jack. He took Annie's hand. They held on to each other and walked through the blowing snow, toward the hut. "Remember Nancy's rules?" said Jack. "There are deep cracks in— AHHH!"

Before Jack could finish, the ground beneath him gave way and he and Annie crashed through a thin layer of snow hiding a deep crack in the ice.

Jack and Annie landed on an icy ledge. Clumps of snow fell on top of them. Silence filled the air. A thin shaft of light came from the opening they had fallen through. It was at least ten feet above them.

"You okay?" Jack said.

"I think so," said Annie.

They both sat up slowly. Annie peered over the edge of the ledge. "Uh-oh," she said. "Look."

Jack looked. He and Annie were on the ledge of a ravine that plunged thousands of feet down into darkness.

"This must be one of those hidden places in the mountain Nancy talked about," said Jack, "the ones made by the lava and hot gases."

"It's incredible," said Annie. She reached into her pocket for her camera.

As soon as Annie moved, Jack heard the ice crack. "Don't move!" he said.

Annie froze.

"Forget pictures," said Jack. "We're facing serious danger here. If we move, the ice might break under us and we'll fall thousands of feet."

"Got it," said Annie. She took a deep breath. "Maybe we should use the wand."

"We can't," said Jack. "The wand won't work. We can only use it for the good of *others*, not just ourselves."

"Darn," said Annie.

They were both still for a moment, listening to the immense silence around them.

"Okay," said Annie. "The way I see it, if we don't use the wand, we'll be stuck here forever. Soon we'll make the wrong move and fall."

"Right," said Jack.

"So we'll never find the secret of happiness for Merlin," said Annie. "Merlin will fade away completely from sorrow. And Camelot will lose his magic forever."

"Right," said Jack.

"So maybe in this case, rescuing ourselves isn't just *our* good," said Annie. "*Our* good is also the good of *others*, like Merlin."

"Good thinking," said Jack. "Let's try it." He carefully twisted around and took off his backpack. Then he very slowly reached inside and pulled out the Wand of Dianthus.

"Okay. Five words . . . ," Jack whispered. "I guess I'll just wish for it to save you and me and Merlin. Hey, why didn't we make that wish a long time ago?"

"We couldn't," said Annie. "We hadn't tried our hardest yet."

"Right. Get ready . . . ," said Jack. He closed his eyes, held up the gleaming silver wand, and said:

"SAVE ANNIE, MERLIN, AND ME!"

Jack waited a moment. Then he opened his eyes and looked around. "What happened?" he said.

"Nothing," said Annie.

"So I guess it didn't work," said Jack. He turned to put the wand away. "I guess the rules must—"

CRACK! The ice broke! The ledge gave way!

"AHHH!" called Jack and Annie as they fell through the twilight, down through darkness,

down,

down,

down,

down into blackness.

CHAPTER SEVEN

The Emperor

Clutching the wand, Jack lay in the pitch-dark. He pushed up his goggles, but he still couldn't see anything.

"You there?" It was Annie's voice.

"Yes," said Jack.

"You okay?"

"Yes. But we're really in trouble now," said Jack. "We fell way down into a dark hole, and the wand doesn't work." He struggled to sit up.

"Well, maybe we should try again," said Annie.

"What's the point?" said Jack. "We'll never get out of here now."

Jack and Annie were silent for a moment.

"Hey—we're moving!" Annie said.

"Moving?" said Jack. They *were* moving. The ice under them was gliding silently and smoothly through the darkness.

"What's happening?" said Jack.

"Maybe we're not in a hole," said Annie. "Look, there's light ahead."

In the distance they saw a glimmer of light. As they kept moving, the light grew brighter. It grew brighter and brighter, until they slipped out of a dark tunnel into dazzling light.

Now Jack could see they were lying on a slab of ice, floating down a narrow river.

"We're on an ice raft!" said Annie.

"What's happening?" said Jack again.

"I don't know," said Annie. "But I think maybe the wand *did* work."

The ice raft floated through light and shadow, past tall frozen cliffs. Then it glided toward an archway in one of the cliff walls.

"Where are we going?" asked Jack.

The raft floated through the archway into a gigantic cavern. The cavern was like a huge icy cathedral. Its walls shone as if they were covered with silver.

"Ohhh," whispered Annie.

"What *is* this place?" said Jack.

"I don't know. But now I'm *sure* the wand worked," said Annie.

The ice raft kept floating along a thin river inside the cavern, past icy archways and jagged ledges. Jack felt as if they were being watched. He thought he heard whispering and breathing.

"*Look!*" said Annie. She pointed to one of the cave openings. Standing on the ledge outside the cave entrance were two penguins. They looked just like the emperor penguins Jack and Annie had seen earlier.

Jack and Annie stood up so they could see better. As their raft floated toward the ledge, the penguin in front stepped back into the cave. The other didn't move.

"*Oh, man!*" said Jack.

The penguin wore a glittering crown.

"The *ancient crown*," Jack whispered. "We found it!"

Annie didn't say anything. She just smiled as the ice raft floated straight toward the emperor penguin. It hit the ledge with a gentle bump.

"Hi," Annie said simply.

The penguin made deep murmuring sounds. He didn't speak in human speech. But somehow Jack and Annie could understand every word: *Welcome to the Cave of the Ancient Crown.*

Annie bowed. The penguin had such dignity, Jack bowed, too.

The emperor spoke again: *Come.* He beckoned with his wing, then turned.

Annie stepped off the ice raft onto the ledge and followed the emperor into the cave. Jack put the Wand of Dianthus into his pack. He hoisted the pack onto his back and tried to balance his weight so he could step from the raft to the ledge.

"Hurry!" said Annie, poking her head out of the cave.

"I'm coming!" said Jack. He leapt from the raft onto the ledge, then hurried into the cave.

The Cave of the Ancient Crown was sparkling. Icicles hung everywhere. Pillars of ice glimmered with blue light. From behind a row of ice pillars came the sound of music—strange music, unlike any Jack had ever heard before. It sounded like the music of a thousand icicle wind chimes.

The emperor led Jack and Annie around the pillars.

"Oh, wow," said Annie.

Penguin couples were dancing to the strange music on a glittering ice rink. Pink and blue lights spilled over the dancers as they gracefully glided and turned. Some penguins danced silently with their eyes closed. Others touched beaks. A group of baby penguins danced together, hopping and sliding on the ice.

"How—how could this be happening?" stammered Jack.

"Don't ask," whispered Annie. "It's magic."

A murmur went through the ballroom as the penguins began to notice Jack and Annie. Though the strange music kept playing, all the dancers came to a stop. None of the penguins seemed alarmed, though. They all looked at their visitors with calm, friendly faces.

The emperor spoke to Jack and Annie: *Word reached us earlier that you saved one of our own. We have been hoping to meet you.*

Puzzled, Jack looked at Annie.

"When we first got here, remember?" she whispered.

"Oh, right," said Jack. He'd forgotten all about rescuing the small penguin from the petrel.

You may stay with us for as long as you wish, said the emperor. *You are honored members of our tribe now.*

"Thank you," said Annie. "But we can't stay

long. We came to Antarctica to look for a secret of happiness."

"To save one of our friends," said Jack. It felt natural to tell the emperor and his tribe the truth. They lived in a world as magical as the world of Camelot. "His name is Merlin. He's the magician of Camelot, and he's really sad."

The penguins began murmuring and whispering to one another. Jack couldn't understand what they were saying. From the back of the crowd, a baby penguin waddled forward, the tiniest one in the tribe.

"Oh, look . . . ," breathed Annie.

Jack grinned from ear to ear. The baby was a fuzzy gray ball with big dark eyes. It was even smaller than the young penguin they had saved from the petrel. The little penguin waddled up to the emperor.

Peep, peep, she said.

The emperor looked down at her.

Peep, peep.

She says she wishes to go with you, said the emperor. *She wants to help your friend.*

"But she's so little!" said Annie. "What about her mom and dad?"

She is an orphan, said the emperor. *Her parents were lost in a terrible storm. But she is very brave and full of joy. I know that she will bring happiness to your friend Merlin.*

Annie turned to the baby penguin. "Thank you," she said. Then she leaned over and patted the penguin's tiny head. "Oh, touch her, Jack. She's so soft."

Jack patted the baby on the head, too. As he touched her soft little feathers, she tilted her head and stared at him with her big eyes. Jack felt a wave of tenderness for the baby penguin. He couldn't believe she was an orphan. Tears came to his eyes, but he quickly blinked them away and cleared his throat. "Thanks, Penny," he said.

Annie giggled. Jack couldn't believe he'd just named the little penguin Penny. Usually Annie was the one who named the animals.

Peep, said Penny.

She would like you to pick her up, said the emperor.

"Oh. Okay," said Jack. He leaned over and held out his arms. Penny snuggled close to his parka.

Peep!

Jack laughed and picked Penny up. He held the little penguin tightly.

The emperor turned to the crowd. He said something Jack couldn't understand. The crowd parted to make a path. The emperor nodded at Jack and Annie. *Let us go now*, he said. As Jack, Annie, and Penny left with the emperor, the penguins flapped their wings against their bodies, applauding.

"Good-bye!" Annie called to the crowd.

Jack smiled and waved.

Peep! said Penny.

The icicle chime music grew softer and softer as Jack and Annie followed the emperor through the cave.

The tall penguin led them outside onto the ledge.

Thank you for your help today, he said.

"Thank *you* for letting Penny come with us," said Annie.

"We promise to take good care of her. We'll take her to Merlin," said Jack.

The emperor touched the orphan's downy head with the tip of his wing. He leaned close to her and softly murmured something in her ear.

Peep, Penny said.

The emperor looked up at Jack and Annie. Silently, he bowed to them and they bowed back. Then the emperor penguin turned and walked back into the Cave of the Ancient Crown.

Jack sighed. For a moment, he hated to leave the enchanted world of the penguins.

"Oh, she's cold, Jack," said Annie.

Jack looked down. Penny was shivering in his arms.

"Put her inside your parka," said Annie.

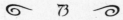

Jack unzipped his parka and carefully placed the little penguin against his sweater. He pulled the zipper back up. He held Penny close to him.

"Perfect," said Annie. "Just make sure she can breathe okay."

"Don't worry," said Jack, patting his jacket. "I'll take good care of her."

"Do you think we can use the wand now to get back?" asked Annie.

Jack nodded. "I think so," he said. "I can't think of any other way."

"Should we tell it to take us to the tree house?" asked Annie. "Or Frog Creek? Or Camelot?"

"No, we have to go back to Mount Erebus first," said Jack. "If Nancy finds out that Pete never picked us up, she really *will* have a heart attack."

"Oh, right," said Annie. "Then we better put on our masks and goggles again."

Jack pulled up his face mask and pulled down his goggles. "Get the wand out of my pack," he said.

Annie reached into Jack's backpack and pulled out the Wand of Dianthus. "Okay, ready?" she said.

Jack patted his parka, comforting the baby penguin. "Here we go, Penny," he said, "on a big adventure."

Annie held up the wand, then took a deep breath and said, "TAKE US BACK TO NANCY!"

In less than an instant, Jack and Annie and Penny were on the slope of Mount Erebus.

CHAPTER EIGHT

A Good Story

The snowmobiles and the helicopter were both parked on the slope. The scientists and journalists stood talking with Nancy and Pete.

"Oh, no!" Annie said, grabbing Jack. "What about Penny? We're not supposed to have a penguin! They'll take her away!"

Jack put his arms protectively over his parka. "I'll hide her," he said. "We've got to get her to Merlin."

Jack heard a shout. He turned around. Nancy had caught sight of them. She was waving her arms and running toward them.

"Hey, you two!" Nancy called. She dashed across the snow and threw her arms around Annie, then Jack.

Jack held his breath, hoping Penny wouldn't be squashed.

Peep.

Jack pulled away from Nancy and pretended to cough. He made his coughing end in a sort of *peep.*

"The chopper just got here!" said Nancy. "Pete told me he was delayed by a snow squall! I freaked out! Where have you been? Are you okay?"

"Don't worry, we're fine," said Annie.

"Perfect," said Jack. "We don't feel a bit sick or anything. We were just getting some fresh air. We're ready to go now!" Jack started walking toward the chopper.

Annie grabbed Nancy's arm and walked with her. "Did you have fun on the mountain?" Annie asked, trying to keep Nancy's attention off Jack. "What happened? What did you see?"

"We saw lots of things, but I was worried about you guys the whole time," said Nancy. "Your parents must be frantic back at the station!"

"They had their own expedition today," said Annie. "They study penguins."

Peep!

"What was that?" asked Nancy.

Jack did his weird cough again.

"Are you sure you're okay, Jack?" Nancy called after him.

"I'm perfect," he said.

As the three of them approached the others, they were greeted with cheers. Nancy must have told everyone that we're just little kids, Jack thought.

"So glad you're safe, young man!" said Ali, the biologist. He slapped Jack on the back.

Penny peeped, and Jack coughed.

"Sorry you couldn't make it up to the top," said Kim, the photographer.

"That's okay," said Annie. "We still got a good story."

"Did you now?" said Lucy, the space scientist.

"Yes, a *really* good story!" said Annie.

"Excellent, but you mustn't tell a soul," said Tony, the journalist, "or one of us will steal it!" Tony laughed, and the others laughed with him.

"Okay, we'll keep it a secret." Annie smiled.

Pete opened the door of the chopper.

"Brave little kids first," said Nancy.

Oh, brother, thought Jack.

Nancy ushered Jack and Annie toward the helicopter. They scrambled up the steps, climbed aboard, and sat down.

As the others climbed in and got settled, Jack loosened his seat belt so he could buckle up without crushing Penny.

Peep!

Jack coughed. But to his relief, Pete started the engine. The rotor blades began to spin.

"Headphones!" yelled Nancy.

Everyone pulled on their headphones.

Nancy gave Jack and Annie a big smile and a thumbs-up sign as the helicopter lifted off the mountain slope.

"I love late spring evenings in Antarctica," Nancy said to the group.

Jack looked out the window. The evening sky was lavender with streaks of pink.

"This light always reminds me that we're in a different world from the world back home," said Nancy.

Jack and Annie smiled at each other. If only the others knew how many different worlds there really were.

The chopper swept up through the soft light of the cold sky,

    up the slope of the burning mountain,

        past the orange-red lake of boiling lava,

            over white fields of ice and snow,

until finally it landed at the heliport, where the red bus was waiting.

The chopper blades stopped spinning. Pete gave the signal. Then Jack and Annie followed Nancy and the others out of the helicopter.

Jack held Penny in place under his parka as he boarded the red bus. He sat with Annie near the back.

Nancy took the driver's seat and started the engine. As the bus rolled along, Jack peeked inside his parka. Penny looked up at him. She blinked a few times, as if she was a little worried. Jack patted her gently until she closed her eyes and fell asleep.

Jack kept patting the front of his parka to comfort Penny. He looked out the window and patted the baby penguin the whole ride. As Penny snuggled close to Jack, none of his worries of the day mattered anymore: his fear of falling into the lava lake, his dread of altitude sickness, his embarrassment at being caught by Nancy. All the cares and confusions of the day were wiped away by his feelings for the orphan penguin.

When the red bus stopped at the station, Jack and Annie followed everyone down the aisle and climbed off. As the others stood talking in a group, Jack and Annie started walking away.

"We're leaving now! Bye, Nancy!" said Annie. "Bye, everyone!"

"Thanks for everything!" called Jack.

"Oh, no you don't!" said Nancy. She grabbed them both by the sleeves of their parkas. "I'm not letting you two out of my sight again, not until I hand-deliver you to your parents."

"But—but ... our parents are still on their penguin expedition," said Annie.

"Then I'll take you to where you're staying," said Nancy. "Come on." Clutching their parkas, she started walking them toward the buildings. "You all must be staying at the wildlife quarters, right?"

"Uh—yes," said Jack.

Nancy led Jack and Annie to a building at the edge of the compound. "Well, here you are. Home safe and sound."

"Thanks!" said Annie.

"Bye!" said Jack. He was desperate to get away with Penny.

"Wait—" said Nancy.

Oh, no. What now? thought Jack.

"I'm still worried about you guys," said Nancy. "Are your parents really here to study penguins? I want you to tell me the true story now."

Annie heaved a sigh. "Okay. The true story is that Jack and I came alone to Antarctica in a magic tree house—"

"Annie!" said Jack.

But Annie kept talking. "It belongs to Morgan le Fay of Camelot. Morgan wants us to find the fourth secret of happiness for Merlin the magician. See, he's very sad. And as soon as we leave Antarctica, we're headed for Camelot to cheer him up."

Nancy just stared at Annie. Jack held his breath, afraid Nancy would finally have her heart attack.

But Nancy burst out laughing and shook her head. "Where did *that* come from?" she said. "You guys are so cute! How do you think up this stuff? Seriously now, tell me the truth."

"Well . . . ," started Jack.

"Oh, look!" said Annie. "Mom! Dad!"

"What?" said Jack.

"There they are!" said Annie. She pointed to a couple bundled up in parkas, goggles, and ski masks. They were walking toward a building.

"Oh—right!" said Jack. "Mom! Dad!"

The couple kept walking and disappeared behind the building.

"They didn't hear us!" said Annie. "We better

go! They'll wonder where we are. Bye, Nancy! Thanks for everything!"

"Nancy, you coming with us for coffee?" Tony yelled, standing by the bus.

"You should go, Nancy," said Annie. "We'll be fine."

"Okay," said Nancy, sighing. "Bye, guys. Run and catch up with your folks."

Peep!

Jack coughed his funny cough.

"And take care of that cough of yours, Jack!" said Nancy.

"Don't worry, I will!" said Jack.

Then Jack and Annie took off. They ran behind the building. They stopped and peeked back around the corner. They watched Nancy walk off with Tony and the others.

"Let's go," said Jack. He and Annie hurried away from all the buildings at McMurdo Station.

Jack put his arms around Penny as they crossed the icy slope and ran to the cliff near the seashore.

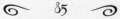

The tree house was still there, tucked under the overhang. Annie climbed in through the window. Jack followed her, careful not to let Penny slip out of his parka.

Annie pulled Morgan's rhyme out of her pocket and read the last part:

> *Then speed to Camelot by close of day,*
> *Lest grief take Merlin forever away.*

"Let's go!" said Jack. "Speed to Camelot!"

Annie pointed to the word *Camelot* and said loudly and clearly: "I wish we could go there!"

A blast of light—

a roar of wind—

a rumble of thunder—

and, of course,

they were *there*.

CHAPTER NINE

Penny and Merlin

*P*_{eep}.

Penny's head was sticking out of Jack's jacket. Jack and Annie were wearing their own clothes again—their jeans, jackets, hats, and scarves. All their heavy cold-weather gear for Antarctica was gone.

"We're in Camelot," said Annie, looking out the window.

Jack took Penny out of his jacket and held her up to the window so she could see the grounds of King Arthur's castle.

The tree house had landed in an apple tree in an orchard. In the near distance, castle towers rose into a late-afternoon sky. Several knights on horses were riding away from the castle.

"Jack! Annie!"

Teddy and Kathleen were running through the orchard, between the trees, over fallen golden leaves and apples.

Jack and Annie waved at them.

"Oh, I just thought of something," said Jack. "We forgot to find out the fourth secret."

"What do you mean?" said Annie. "It's Penny."

"No, I don't think so," said Jack. "Remember, Leonardo da Vinci told us a secret of happiness has to be available to everyone. Not many people can have their own baby penguin."

"Oh, right," said Annie.

"Jack! Annie! Come down!" Teddy and Kathleen called from below.

"We're coming!" said Annie.

Jack put Penny inside his jacket, then carefully

climbed down the rope ladder after Annie.

"Oh! What did you bring back with you?" said Kathleen.

Penny was peeking out of Jack's jacket again. "A baby penguin for Merlin," said Annie.

"Look at her!" said Kathleen. "She's beautiful!"

"Indeed!" said Teddy, petting Penny's downy head.

Peep.

"She wants to help Merlin," said Annie.

"Then let us hurry to him at once," said Teddy. "Come, follow us."

Kathleen and Teddy led the way between the trees to a small wooden cottage at the edge of the orchard.

"Merlin's in *there*?" asked Jack.

"'Tis a garden house he always loved as a child," said Teddy. "Morgan thought he would find comfort there. But alas, he seems to have found nothing but more grief. He will eat nothing, and he has not spoken for days."

Teddy opened the door to the cottage and ushered Annie and Jack inside.

Morgan was sitting by Merlin's bed. Late-afternoon light slanted through the window onto the magician's face. He lay very still. His eyes were closed and his hands were folded on his chest.

A chill went through Jack. Merlin hardly looked alive.

Morgan turned around. She, too, looked tired, but her face brightened when she saw Jack and Annie. "Thank goodness you have come!" she said.

Annie crossed the room and hugged Morgan. Jack stepped forward with Penny. "Look what we brought for Merlin," he whispered.

"Oh!" said Morgan. The enchantress gently touched the little penguin. "She is lovely indeed," she whispered. "Thank you for bringing her."

Morgan turned back to Merlin. "Merlin?" she said. "Jack and Annie from Frog Creek are here. They want to talk with you."

Annie stepped forward, while Jack stood in the shadows with Penny. "Hi, Merlin!" said Annie. "How are you doing?"

The magician didn't open his eyes. But he nodded to let Annie know he heard her.

"We have four secrets of happiness to share with you," said Annie. She reached into Jack's backpack. She pulled out the poem that the poet Basho had given them on their trip to old Japan.

"Listen, here's a poem from a man named Basho," said Annie. She read the short poem:

> *An old pond:*
> *a frog jumps in—*
> *the sound of water.*

"The secret of happiness for Basho was that he paid attention to small things in nature," explained Annie.

Merlin nodded slowly. "Nature," he said in a raspy voice.

"That's right," said Annie. "And we brought

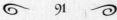

you this, too." She pulled out the angel picture Leonardo da Vinci had drawn. She held it up to show Merlin.

"This is an angel drawn by a great genius named Leonardo da Vinci," said Annie.

Merlin opened his eyes and peered at the drawing.

"Isn't she beautiful?" said Annie. "The secret of Leonardo's happiness was that he had great curiosity about everything—angels, art, noses, feathers, flowers, flying. Every day he felt happy when he learned something new."

Merlin nodded as he stared at the angel sketch. "Curiosity," he breathed.

"Yes. And here's the third secret," said Annie. She reached into Jack's pack and pulled out the nautilus shell they'd been given on their trip to the deep ocean.

"A sea creature once lived inside this shell," said Annie. "We learned from an ocean scientist that a secret of happiness is having compassion for all living things, from a tiny shell creature to a giant octopus."

Merlin took the shell from Annie. He cupped his hands around it and closed his eyes. His face softened. "Compassion," he said. But still he didn't smile.

Jack sighed. *Maybe Merlin isn't going to get better,* he thought.

"Give him Penny now, Jack," whispered Annie.

Jack stepped out from the shadows.

"Merlin," he said, "we don't actually know what the fourth secret of happiness is, but we want to give you something else."

Merlin looked at Jack.

Jack held up the tiny penguin. "Her name is Penny," he said.

Merlin just stared at Penny. He looked confused.

"She's an orphan," said Jack. "Her parents were lost in a terrible storm."

Merlin frowned. "She is very small," he said hoarsely.

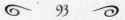

"Yes. And she wants to live with you," said Annie.

"The emperor of the Cave of the Ancient Crown wants you to take care of her," said Jack. "He says she is very brave and full of joy."

Jack set Penny on the floor. Standing alone, the penguin looked tiny and fragile.

"Go to Merlin," Jack urged Penny.

Penny waddled across the floor to Merlin. Her little body rocked stiffly from side to side as she held out her wings to keep her balance.

Penny stopped in front of Merlin. The little penguin and the old magician stared at each other for a moment. Merlin's expression didn't change.

Peep! said Penny. *Peep! Peep!*

Merlin's face twitched. Then he began to laugh. At first his laughter seemed more like coughing than laughing, as if he hadn't laughed in a long time. But then his laughter grew louder. He stood up and scooped the baby penguin into his arms.

Merlin hugged Penny to his chest, pressing her against his long white beard. His face settled into a warm smile.

"It is your destiny to care for her, Merlin," said Morgan. "The emperor of the Cave of the Ancient Crown has sent her to you. He is very wise."

Merlin nodded. Then, cradling Penny in his arms, he walked to the doorway of the cottage and looked out. "The air smells like ripe apples and wood smoke today," he said.

"Yes, my old friend, it does," said Morgan. She wiped tears from her eyes.

Merlin turned back and looked at Jack and Annie. "Thank you for bringing— What did you say her name was?"

"Penny," said Annie.

"Ah, yes, *Penny* . . . to me," said Merlin. "And thank you for your other gifts as well. I will never forget the secrets you have shared with me."

"You're welcome," said Jack and Annie.

Peep.

"Yes, yes," Merlin murmured to the baby penguin. "You will stay with me. And we will have a happy time together. Let us go into the orchard and I will show you the rising moon."

Merlin put Penny down on the ground. The baby penguin took tiny quick steps alongside the magician as they walked into the orchard. The two strolled together between the trees, and a round moon rose over the kingdom of Camelot.

CHAPTER TEN

The Secret

"Well done," Teddy said softly.

"Indeed," said Kathleen, smiling at Jack and Annie.

Morgan smiled at them, too. "Thank you for your four secrets," she said.

"You're welcome," said Annie. "But we're not exactly sure what the fourth secret is."

"I told Annie I don't think it can be a baby penguin," said Jack. "Because in our time people aren't allowed to have baby penguins."

"That is true," said Morgan. "But people can

always take care of someone—or some creature—
who needs them."

"So *that's* the secret?" said Annie.

Morgan nodded. "Taking loving care of another
can make one very happy," she said. "Like the
other three secrets, it helps us look outside ourselves. Then we can better see all the gifts the
world has to offer."

"Yeah, taking care of Penny really took my
attention off myself," Jack said. "I forgot about a
million things I was worried about."

"I know you will miss her," said Morgan. "But
I imagine you will see her again someday."

"So are we going on another mission soon?"
asked Annie.

"Return home and rest first, and we will send
for you again," said Morgan.

"Can you try to make it really soon?" said
Annie. "We don't like long rests."

Morgan laughed. "We will see," she said.

"Oh, before we leave, I want to take a picture

of you three guys," said Annie. "It's for my family project at school. You seem like a family to me. Look this way, please."

Annie aimed her camera at Morgan, Teddy, and Kathleen. "Smile!" she said.

"What are you doing?" asked Teddy. "What are you holding?"

"It's a camera," said Annie. "Just smile. Say *cheese*."

"Cheese? Why 'cheese'?" said Teddy.

Click! Flash!

"Got it." Annie put her camera back into her pocket.

"What was that? What did you do?" asked Teddy.

"It's hard to explain," said Jack. "It's like magic. From our time."

"Good-bye now," said Morgan, smiling. "Have a safe journey home to *your* family."

"Thanks," said Jack.

"See all you guys again soon—*real* soon, we hope!" said Annie.

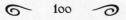

"We hope so, too!" said Teddy.

"Good-bye," said Kathleen.

Jack and Annie left the garden cottage and hurried back to the tree house.

They climbed up the rope ladder. Jack grabbed the Pennsylvania book and opened it to a picture of the Frog Creek woods.

"Wait, I see Merlin and Penny! Look!" Annie pointed toward Merlin in the distance. He was still walking through the apple orchard with Penny at his side.

"They look like a little family now, too," said Jack.

"Yeah, they do. I should take their picture," said Annie. She aimed her camera at Merlin and Penny and took a picture. Then she sighed. "Okay, home now."

"Bye, Penny," Jack said softly. Then he pointed in the book to the words *Frog Creek*. "I wish we could go there!" he said.

The wind started to blow.

The tree house started to spin.

It spun faster and faster.

Then everything was still.

Absolutely still.

"We're home," Annie said. "That was a great trip." She and Jack were back in the Frog Creek woods.

"Yeah. I hope we see Penny on our next mission," said Jack.

"If we see Merlin, we'll probably see Penny," said Annie. "I think those two are a team now. At least we have a picture of them—and a picture of Teddy, Kathleen, and Morgan."

Annie held up her camera and clicked through the photo display. "Oh, no!" she said. "I don't believe it!"

"What?" said Jack.

"All my pictures are gone!" said Annie. "No Antarctica! No Merlin or Morgan! No penguins!"

"Really?" said Jack. "Maybe you can't keep the pictures you take on a magical trip."

"I think you're right," said Annie. "I only have

one picture. I took it right before we left home."
She held up her camera to show Jack. It was a picture of him. He had a grin on his face.

"That's when I saw the streak of light over the woods," said Jack, "and I knew the tree house was back."

"Well, at least I captured *that* moment," said Annie, sighing.

"Yep." Jack put the Antarctica book on the floor of the tree house and pulled on his pack. Then he climbed down the rope ladder. Annie followed. As they started tramping over the fallen leaves, the woods were growing dark. Jack felt a little cold and hungry.

"So the fourth secret is *take care of someone who needs you*," said Annie. "I guess that could mean lots of things. Like take care of a sad person, a baby, a puppy, or a new kid in school . . ."

Jack nodded. "Yep," he said. "And maybe it works the other way, too."

"What do you mean?" said Annie.

"I think sometimes you can make other people happy by letting *them* take care of *you*," Jack said.

"Oh, right," said Annie. "It seems to make Mom and Dad happy to take care of us."

"Like when they tell us to wear scarves and gloves," said Jack.

"And make us dinner," said Annie.

"And tell us to be home before dark," said Jack.

"We better hurry," said Annie.

"Yep, let's go make Mom and Dad happy—" said Jack, laughing.

"By letting them take care of us!" said Annie.

The wind shook the tree limbs, and leaves fluttered to the ground. Geese honked overhead as Jack and Annie hurried home through the chilly November twilight.

More Facts About Antarctica

- Today Antarctica is the fifth-largest continent in the world.
- The land area of Antarctica is more than 5 million square miles.
- More than 99 percent of Antarctica is covered with thick ice.
- Ninety percent of all the world's ice can be found in Antarctica.
- In winter, the sea around Antarctica freezes and the continent becomes much bigger.
- Much of the land is unreachable by humans in winter.

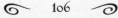

• Mount Erebus is the most active volcano in Antarctica, with daily eruptions.

• Mount Erebus was named after Erebus, a god from Greek mythology who was the son of Chaos. Erebus was the god of darkness, and Antarctica is in darkness for much of the year.

• The continent of Antarctica was first seen by humans less than 200 years ago.

• In the twentieth century, more than forty permanent stations were built in Antarctica by people from many countries.

• For over fifty years, the United States has had a full-time research site called McMurdo Station.

More Facts About Penguins

• There are six kinds of penguins in Antarctica: the Adélie, chinstrap, gentoo, macaroni, king, and emperor.

• Only emperor penguins can winter on Antarctica, because only they can survive the cold.

• In the winter, thousands of emperor penguins march inland and create colonies on the ice of Antarctica. There the female penguin lays her egg. Then she marches north back to the sea to get food for her chick.

• While the female is gone, the male penguin stays with the egg and protects it from the brutal weather. For the next two months, the male penguins all huddle together against the howling winds. Not until their mates finally return do the hungry males head to the sea to eat.

Want to learn more about penguins and Antarctica?

Get the facts behind the fiction in the Magic Tree House® Research Guide.

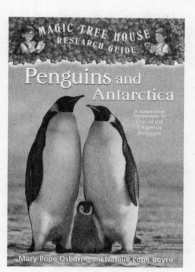

Available now!

Coming in Spring 2009

Don't miss Magic Tree House #41
(A Merlin Mission)

Moonlight on the Magic Flute

Jack and Annie now have to bring happiness
to *millions* of people. How will they do it?

Mary Pope Osborne is the award-winning author of many novels, picture books, story collections, and nonfiction books. Her bestselling Magic Tree House series has been translated into many languages around the world. Highly recommended by parents and educators everywhere, the series introduces young readers to different cultures and times in history, as well as to the world's legacy of ancient myth and storytelling. Mary Pope Osborne is married to Will Osborne, a co-author of many of the Magic Tree House Research Guides and librettist and lyricist for *Magic Tree House: The Musical*, a theatrical adaptation of the series. They live in northwestern Connecticut with their Norfolk terriers, Joey and Mr. Bezo. You can visit Mary, Will, and even Joey and Mr. Bezo on the Web at www.marypopeosborne.com.

Sal Murdocca is best known for his amazing work on the Magic Tree House series. He has written and/or illustrated over two hundred children's books, including *Dancing Granny* by Elizabeth Winthrop, *Double Trouble in Walla Walla* by Andrew Clements, and *Big Numbers* by Edward Packard. He has taught writing and illustration at the Parsons School of Design in New York. He is the librettist for a children's opera and has recently completed his second short film. Sal Murdocca is an avid runner, hiker, and bicyclist. He has often bicycle-toured in Europe and has had many one-man shows of his paintings from these trips. He lives and works with his wife, Nancy, in New City, New York.